THOMAS & FRIENDS™

DAY OF THE DIESELS

Illustrated by Tommy Stubbs

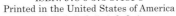 A GOLDEN BOOK · NEW YORK

Thomas the Tank Engine & Friends™

CREATED BY BRITT ALLCROFT

Based on The Railway Series by The Reverend W Awdry.
© 2011 Gullane (Thomas) LLC.
Thomas the Tank Engine & Friends and Thomas & Friends are trademarks of Gullane (Thomas) Limited.
HIT and the HIT Entertainment logo are trademarks of HIT Entertainment Limited.
All rights reserved. Published in the United States by Golden Books, an imprint of Random House Children's Books, a division of
Random House, Inc., 1745 Broadway, New York, NY 10019, and in Canada by Random House of Canada Limited, Toronto.
Golden Books, A Golden Book, A Big Golden Book, and the G colophon are registered trademarks of Random House, Inc.
www.randomhouse.com/kids   www.thomasandfriends.com
ISBN: 978-0-375-87181-8
Printed in the United States of America
10 9 8 7 6 5 4 3 2 1
Random House Children's Books supports the First Amendment and celebrates the right to read.

It was a beautiful day on the Island of Sodor. The sun shone brightly. Thomas and Percy were enjoying a ride in the country. Their steam floated fluffy and white into the cloudless sky.

But as they chuffed around a corner, Thomas and Percy gasped. There was black smoke on the horizon. They raced to find out what was the matter.

Bells rang! Sirens whined! An old farm shed was ablaze. Flames flickered and flashed into the sky. Eager to help, Thomas and Percy let firefighters and farmhands take buckets of water from their tanks.

"We must put out this fire," said Sir Topham Hatt.

"We'll do our best," peeped Thomas.

But the fire rose higher, and the engines were nearly out of water. Suddenly, a new engine named Belle arrived. She was big and blue. Her brass bell banged and clanged.

"Buffer up, Belle!" shouted Sir Topham Hatt. "We need your water!"

Water shot from two spouts high on Belle's water tanks. The flames fizzled and crackled . . . and went out.

Belle was low on water, so Thomas and Percy had to help her to the Steamworks. Victor and Kevin gave Belle special care because she was a hero.

"I've never seen a blue fire engine before," Kevin said.

"That's because I'm not a real fire engine," Belle peeped.

"You are a Really Useful Engine, Belle," said Sir Topham Hatt, "but we need a real fire engine."

Belle had an idea. "Sir, you need Flynn the Fire Engine. He's fast and fearless! He's a real hero."

Thomas and Percy gasped. Victor wheeshed and Kevin wobbled.

"Quite right, Belle," Sir Topham Hatt agreed. "Flynn will come to Sodor. He will be our fire engine."

The next day, Thomas took Belle on a tour of the
Island of Sodor. First, they visited Brendam Docks.
Even rusty old Cranky liked Belle.

Later, they visited Knapford Station and Thomas'
Branch Line. It was a wonderful day. Belle was very
impressed with everything she saw.

Percy watched Thomas and Belle roll back to the Steamworks. He wondered why they hadn't invited him to join them on the tour. Suddenly, Diesel slid up next to him.

"Thomas is very busy with that new blue engine," Diesel hissed.

Percy's firebox fizzled. "I guess he is."

Belle rolled up and introduced herself to Diesel. "Do the Diesels have a place as grand as the Steamworks?"

"Our Dieselworks is not like this at all," Diesel said.

"I'd love to visit," Belle puffed.

Then Thomas arrived, his rods rattling. "Steamies don't go to the Dieselworks. It's dark and dirty, and Diesels can be devious."

Diesel snorted goodbye and slipped away.

The next morning, Sir Topham Hatt gave Percy a special job.
"Flynn the Fire Engine will arrive soon, Percy. This is his hose.
Please deliver it safely to the Sodor Search and Rescue Center."

Percy puffed away proudly. At the edge of the Docks, Diesel oiled up next to him. "I told my friend Diesel 10 about you, Percy. He'd like you to visit the Dieselworks. You'd be his special guest."

"Are you sure, Diesel?" Percy peeped.

Diesel smiled. "I'm very sure, Percy."

Percy wasn't sure he should go to the Dieselworks. Thomas always said Steamies shouldn't puff there—but Thomas didn't seem to care what Percy did these days.

Percy wanted friends who had time for him. He wanted to be a special visitor.

So wheel turn by wheel turn, Percy puffed to the Dieselworks. It glowed a fiery red in the distance. His axles tingled.

Diesel 10 met Percy at the door of the Dieselworks.

"Hello, Percy!" he boomed. "What an honor. Please come in."

The Dieselworks was grimy and filled with clanking furnaces. There were engines Percy knew, like Salty and Mavis, but he met new engines, too. Den and Dart ran the Dieselworks and fixed the Diesels. Percy wanted them to like him, so he told a joke.

"What do you call a train that has a cold?"

No one knew.

"An *achoo*-choo train," Percy peeped.

All the Diesels laughed. Percy was happy that they liked him, but it was getting late.

"I'd love to stay, but I must puff on," Percy said. "I'm supposed to deliver the hose for the new fire engine to the Sodor Search and Rescue Center."

"Dart can take care of that for you," Diesel 10 hissed. Dart uncoupled Percy's flatbed and took it away.

All the Diesels were being so nice. Percy didn't think it was fair that they should stay in such dirty, dingy place. "You should tell Sir Topham Hatt that you need a new Dieselworks," he puffed.

"He doesn't listen to Diesels, only Steamies," said Diesel 10.

Suddenly, an idea flew into Percy's funnel. "I can ask Thomas to tell Sir Topham Hatt. He always listens to Thomas."

Diesel 10 smiled.

Percy went looking for Thomas. He found him at the Steamworks—with Flynn the Fire Engine. Flynn was bright and red and everyone was very impressed, especially Thomas.

Before Percy could tell Thomas about the Dieselworks, Thomas chugged off to show Flynn around Sodor. He didn't even notice Percy.

Percy's boiler bubbled. He felt very unimportant indeed.

The next morning, Percy went back to the Steamworks. Only Kevin was there, but he was excited to hear all about the Dieselworks.

"They don't even have a crane," Percy peeped.

"Victor always says you can't fix an engine without a crane," Kevin said.

"Kevin, if you went there, you'd be a hero," Percy puffed. "They need you."

Kevin liked the idea of being a hero very much.

Suddenly, Thomas whooshed in. "Percy, I've been looking for you. Flynn's hose is missing!"

"It must be at the Search and Rescue Center," Percy said. "A friend delivered it for me."

Percy wanted Thomas to ask him who his friend was, but he didn't. Thomas told Percy to find the hose, then steamed away.

Percy searched until nighttime, but he didn't find the hose. He was starting to worry, but then Percy saw something that really troubled him—Flynn was in *his* berth at Tidmouth Sheds! Percy decided not to stay where he wasn't wanted.

Percy found Kevin, and together they went to the
Dieselworks. The Diesels were very happy to see them.
Percy and Kevin stayed at the Dieselworks all night—
something no Steamie had ever done before.

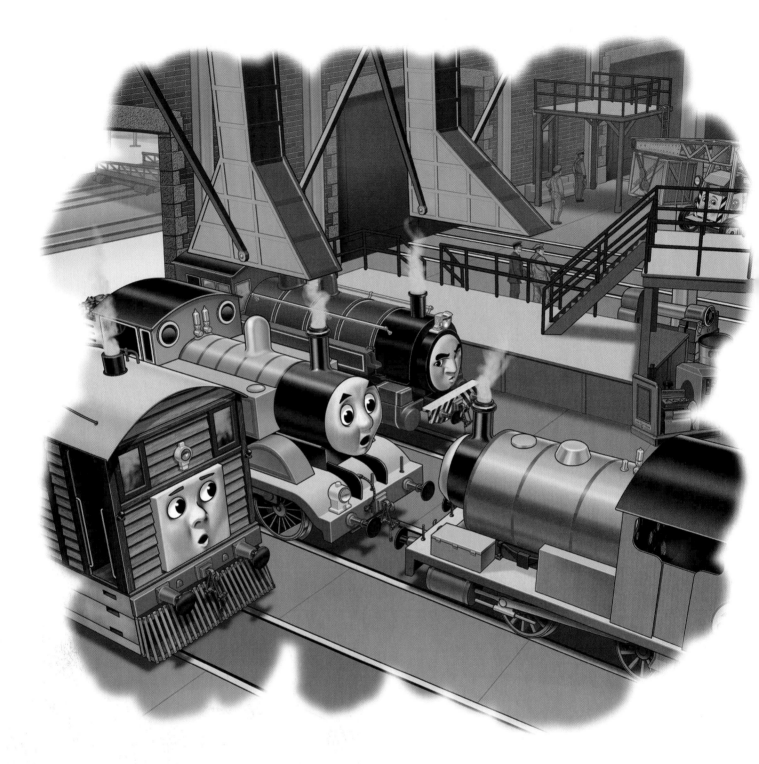

The next morning, Percy told the Steamies where he had
been all night. Everyone was amazed. Toby gasped. Thomas'
firebox fizzled. Victor was angry that Kevin was still at the
Dieselworks.

"I need Kevin here!" Victor raged, then rattled off to tell Sir
Topham Hatt.

Percy was excited that everyone was finally listening to him.

Percy took Thomas to the Dieselworks. Percy was certain that once Thomas saw how dirty and grimy it was, he'd talk to Sir Topham Hatt about the Diesels' troubles.

But Diesel 10 had other plans. "Since Victor is not at the Steamworks, we're going to take it over . . . and we want you to lead us, Percy. You will be our hero!"

Percy felt grander than Gordon and more special than Spencer. He and the Diesels rolled away, leaving a very angry Thomas behind.

Percy proudly puffed ahead of the Diesels. But when they reached the Steamworks, nobody listened to him.

"Out of my way, you silly Steamie!" Diesel 10 roared. "The Steamworks is ours now—and we're not giving it back."

The Diesels roared and raced. They twirled on the turntable and biffed into buffers. And worst of all, Diesel 10 said Thomas was their prisoner at the Dieselworks!

Percy knew he had made a terrible mistake! Thomas was truly his best friend. He had to help him. Percy raced to the Dieselworks and screeched to a stop. Sparks flew up from his wheels and fell on a pile of oily paper. Thomas was nowhere to be found.

The papers burst into flame and the flames spread across the Dieselworks.

Now Percy had to put out a fire, too!

Percy raced to the Search and Rescue Center. Fiery Flynn was ready to race to the rescue—but he didn't have his hose!

"Of course, Dart didn't deliver the hose!" Percy wheeshed. "I've been such a silly Steamie. The hose must still be at the Dieselworks."

With pistons pumping and bells clanging, Percy and Flynn raced to the fire.

Back at the Dieselworks, smoke swirled into the sky. Percy found Den and Dart in an old shed out back—and they were blocking Thomas in! Diesel 10 had told them not to let Thomas go, but they knew they had to help fight the fire.

Den and Dart released Thomas. Then Dart showed Percy where he'd hidden Flynn's hose behind the old shed.

"Stay calm," Flynn thundered. "There's no cause for alarm."
Belle and Flynn faced the fire, and the water flowed fast.
The flames hissed and fizzled. Smoke whirled and twirled.

"Hooray for Flynn!" Thomas peeped.
"Hooray for Belle!" peeped Percy.
The flames grew smaller and smaller and slowly faded.
The Dieselworks was saved! Now it was time to save the Steamworks.

Thomas and Percy knew that friends are strongest when they stick together. As they rolled to the Steamworks, they collected their friends—Belle, Edward, Henry, Gordon, James, Toby, and Emily.

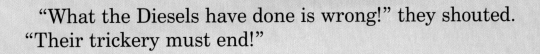

"What the Diesels have done is wrong!" they shouted.
"Their trickery must end!"

The Diesels were surprised to see the Steamies, but they refused to leave the Steamworks.

"Taking things and using trickery is wrong," Thomas peeped. "We can help you get a new Dieselworks, but you have to be fair with us—and we promise not to trick you."

Suddenly, Sir Topham Hatt entered the Steamworks. He was very, very cross.

"Diesel 10," he said sternly. "You are an engine on my railway! You have caused confusion and delay. Because of you, none of my engines has been Really Useful."

Diesel 10 whimpered and winced. His claw crumpled.

Thomas explained why Diesel 10 had been so bad.

"Of course the Diesels will have a new Dieselworks," said Sir Topham Hatt. "That was always my plan. Everything takes time. And everyone must wait their turn."

The Diesels and the Steamies worked together to build the new Dieselworks. Thomas and Percy were happy to work side by side.

Sir Topham Hatt gave Diesel 10 some extra work to do. "No engine on my railway behaves as badly as you did," said Sir Topham Hatt. "You will put right everything you damaged at the Steamworks—and Kevin will be your boss."

At last the new Dieselworks was finished. Everyone came together for the grand opening.

"The new Dieselworks is special because it shows what can happen when all kinds of Really Useful engines work together," said Sir Topham Hatt.

"You are all very special engines," said Sir Topham Hatt. "I'm proud of you."

Percy said he was proudest when he was with Thomas.

"That's exactly how I feel when I'm with you," Thomas peeped.

The two best friends giggled and jiggled and puffed with joy.

In the early 1940s, a loving father crafted a small blue wooden engine for his son, Christopher. The stories that this father, the Reverend W Awdry, made up to accompany the wonderful toy were first published in 1945. Reverend Awdry continued to create new adventures and characters until 1972, when he retired from writing.

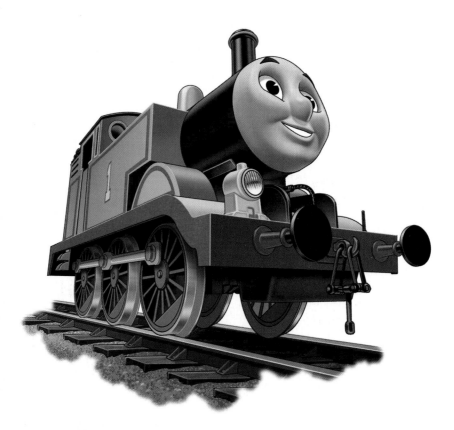

Tommy Stubbs has been an illustrator for several decades. Lately, he has been illustrating the newest tales of Thomas and his engine friends, including *May the Best Engine Win!; Thomas and the Great Discovery; Hero of the Rails;* and *Misty Island Rescue.*